For Peter and Peter
B.D.
For Rosemary, my parents
and everyone at Walker Books
I.A.

First published 1998 by Walker Books Ltd
87 Vauxhall Walk, London SE11 5HJ

2 4 6 8 10 9 7 5 3 1

Text © 1998 Berlie Doherty
Illustrations © 1998 Ian Andrew

This book has been typeset in Tiepolo Bold.

Printed in Italy

British Library Cataloguing in Publication Data
A catalogue record for this book is
available from the British Library.

ISBN 0-7445-6110-8

The Midnight Man

BERLIE DOHERTY

ILLUSTRATED BY **IAN ANDREW**

WALKER BOOKS
AND SUBSIDIARIES
LONDON · BOSTON · SYDNEY

Every night, when Harry and Mister Dog
are asleep, someone comes riding by.

Mister Dog opens one eye and grunts.

Harry opens one eye and yawns.

They both sit up

and gaze out of the window,

and this is what they see...

The midnight man comes
riding through the town
on his midnight horse
with its hushing hooves.
His cloak of whispers
swirls around like sighs.
On his hip is a sack of stars.

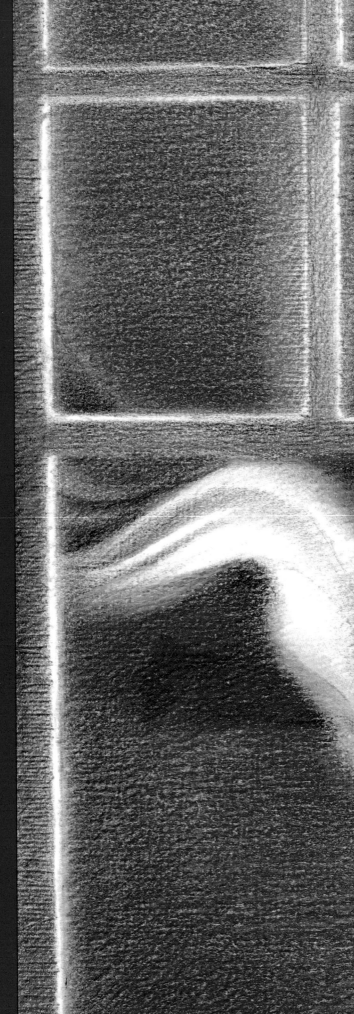

He pauses, and his horse nods its head and waits.

Then he flings the stars far up to the deep dark sky

and there they hang and glitter like flowers of ice.

And some come sprinkling over Mister Dog,

round his nose, and make him sneeze.

And some brush against Harry's face and dust his eyes.

"Who is it?" whispers Harry.

"Woof!" woofs Mister Dog.

 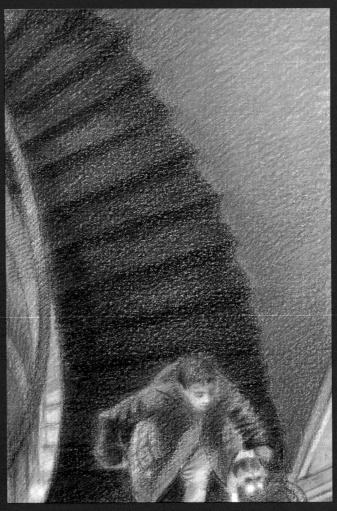

They tiptoe downstairs, past all the snoring doors,

and they're out and up the street

before the latch clicks shut.

The midnight man goes riding on his midnight horse
and all the black shadow-cats slink around
his midnight-quiet hooves.

"Wait for me!" Harry shouts, but his voice is soft as mist
and his feet make sounds like hushes on the ground.
"Woof!" woofs Mister Dog,
but his woof has turned to shush
and his paws are faint as feathers
as he trots along behind.

"You can't come with me!" the midnight man laughs.
His voice is like owl-cries and fox-calls far away.

But still they call, and still they run,
and still they make no sound ...
down the streets and over bridges,
under arches, through the trees,

till they come to the last house
at the very end of town
where the moors stretch into darkness
as if there's no world left.

And softer and fainter go the pittering midnight hooves.

"No resting-place for me. My home is midnight land."

and once he waves his hand.

Harry and Mister Dog lie sleeping on the ground

where the moors stretch away to the end of the world.

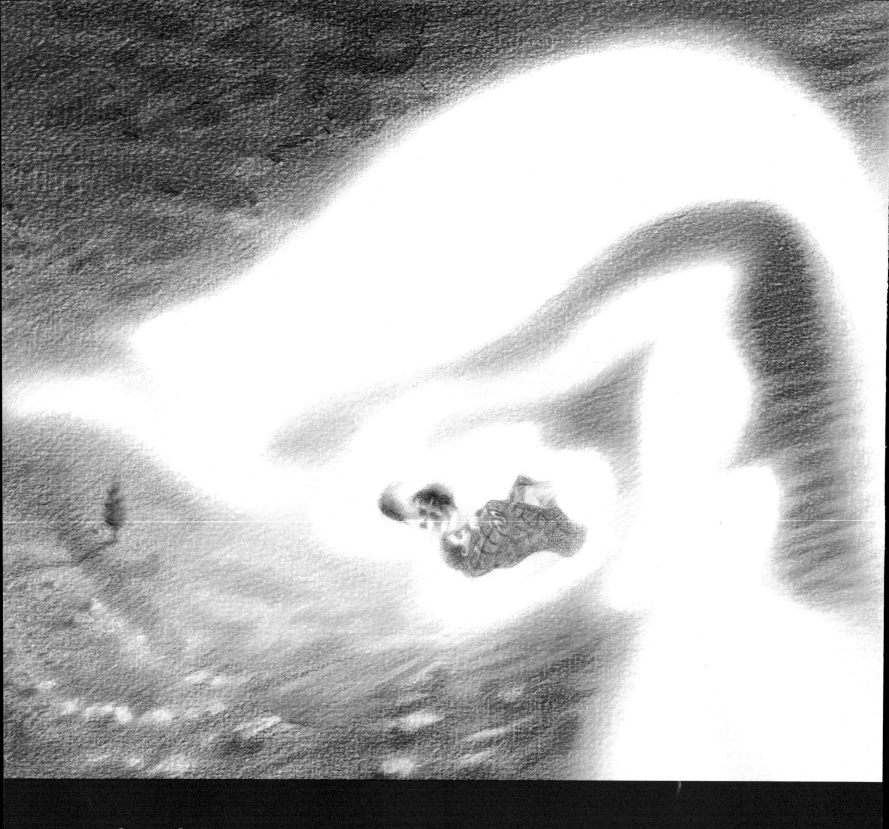

But the white moon sees as she swings across the sky.

She slides down the darkness and peers at them and cries.

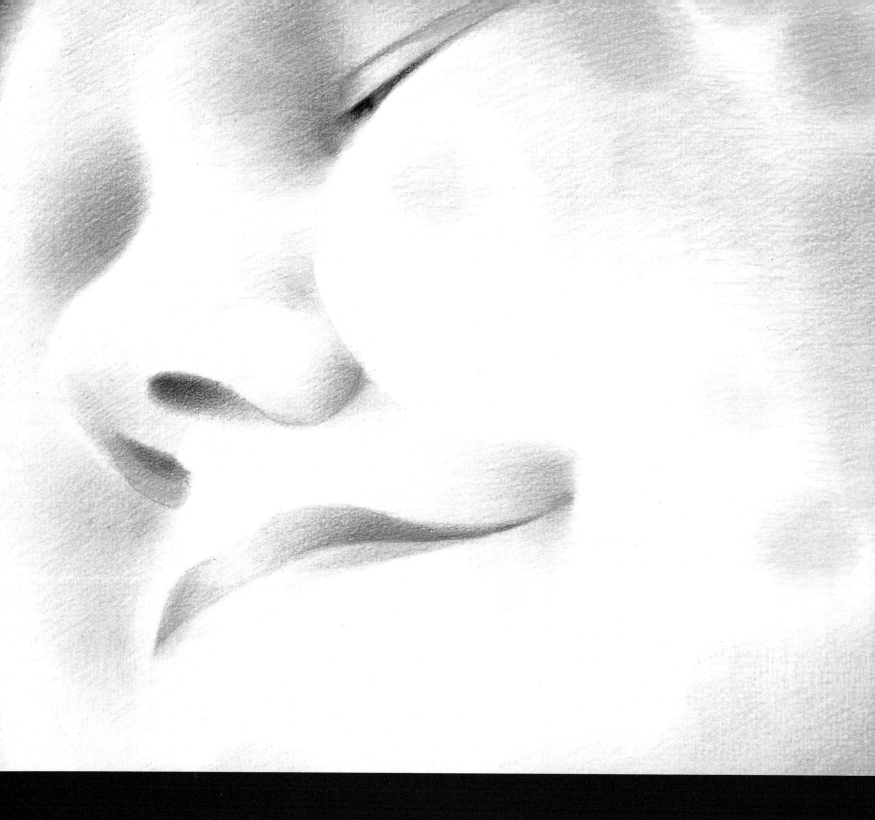

She cradles them into her creamy arms and sways back
through the trees where the midnight man had been...

Under arches, over bridges, down the streets,

past the slinking shadow-cats

to the door of Harry's house,

with the latch clicked shut.

She streams through the window,

and glides up the tiptoe stairs

and folds them down

into their tousled beds.

Mister Dog opens one eye and grunts.

Harry opens one eye and yawns.

They seem to see a winking moon

slipping through the starry sky.

They seem to hear a midnight horse

galloping on midnight hooves.

And do they hear a midnight voice,

laughing like owl-cries and fox-calls,

from far across the world...

"Midnight man!" says Harry.

"Woof!" woofs Mister Dog.

They brush the star dust from their eyes
and sleep till morning comes.